ALANA GRAY

Lumber and Lace

First edition

ISBN: 978-1-0698120-8-7

This book was professionally typeset on Reedsy.
Find out more at reedsy.com

Contents

Free Book!

Scan the QR code to see a full book list and subscribe to my newsletter

Alana Gray

Lumber and Lace

I was playing with fire, and for someone who worked with timber, that was dangerous.

Layne

I dodged a bullet. Calling off my wedding was the easy part. Leaving my high-powered finance career to regroup in a quiet mountain town was the reset I desperately needed. Now I'm managing my brother Jace's log home company and living in a small cabin he built, trying to figure out who I am without a fiancé or a five-year plan.

There's just one loose end I can't escape.

My ex refuses to let go, and I still need to untangle the last threads of our shared life.

Enter Elias.

My brother's employee and friend. All flannel, sawdust, and

steady calm. He offers to play the role of my new boyfriend long enough to convince my ex to finally back off. It's supposed to be simple, temporary and, most importantly, fake.

Except my fake boyfriend is showing up for me in ways my real fiancé never did. And the more I lean on him, the harder it becomes to remember why this is only an act.

Elias

I've had feelings for Layne since the day I met her. I just never thought I'd get the chance to act on them.

Now she's back in town, working alongside me, and trusting me to be her knight in shining armor, when I'm usually just some guy in steel toed boots. Pretending to be her boyfriend seems harmless. Helpful, even. A few staged encounters, a few convincing kisses, and her ex is gone for good.

But pretending gets complicated fast when every smile feels real and every touch leaves me wanting more.

She's my boss's sister. She's fresh out of a broken engagement. Besides, with her protective brother signing my paychecks, falling for her could cost me everything.

The problem is, I don't want to stop.

Is there a way to make this work… or am I digging myself a hole I can't climb out of?

Chapter One

Layne

I guess there's no such thing as a clean break.

Not when we'd been together as long as Teddy and I had.

I paced back and forth in my living room. Well, my borrowed living room. I was living in a one-room cabin my brother Jace had built in the small town of Wildrose Bend outside of Springwood, BC, trying to get my life back together after calling off my wedding.

"The next thing we need to figure out is our car insurance. I'm on yours, you're on mine. We'll need to go to the insurance place together to make the change."

He sighed. "Layne, I understood when you moved your stuff out of the house. I accepted it when you forwarded your mail, but don't you think this is going a little far?"

I rubbed my temple. "No, it's not. We split up. Why would you need insurance to drive my car when we aren't a couple?"

"Babe, come on. We both know this isn't permanent."

"I broke up with you on our wedding day. I lost thousands of dollars, we both did. You think I'd do that if I wasn't sure what I wanted?" I wouldn't, not with how the guilt was eating at me now.

He laughed.

Actually, laughed.

He was such an arrogant ass. How could I not have seen it before?

I ran my hand over the smooth top of the wooden table my brother had built for this place.

"All couples fight," he said with a nonchalance that had my blood pressure rising. "Besides, you can't tell me you prefer working with the lumberjacks instead of in finance. Was your MBA just a waste of money?"

I forced myself to breathe through the anger and the guilt. Teddy and I had met working for my dad's finance company. Dad couldn't just fire Teddy because he and I broke up, so I'd left. Teddy seemed to take my silence as an admission and kept going. "This isn't you, Layne, you want more than this small-town redneck shit."

Internally screaming.

I had told myself a hundred times that arguing with him got me nowhere, but man, he made it hard some days. As I was about to lay into him, there was a knock at my door.

"Hang on."

I crossed the smooth wooden floor and opened the door without looking. I expected it was either my brother or my best friend Sloane coming to check on me. The two of them were a couple now, so they didn't surface from the bedroom often, but when they did, it was to hover over me like mother hens.

Surprisingly, it was neither of them.

Chapter One

"Elias, hey." I stepped back to let all six-plus feet of him walk through my door. The cabin barely felt big enough to hold him. A cold blast of air came in with him and I slammed the door against it.

He looked the same as always in a thick winter jacket layered over plaid flannel and jeans, dirt-streaked and smelling of pine. He was broad and thick, had the body of a man who was over forty and had probably spent thirty of those years working his ass off at a physical job. On the other hand, he kept his hair and beard buzzed almost to the skin and he wore thick-framed nerdy glasses.

I shouldn't be noticing those things.

It was too soon after my breakup with Teddy.

I also shouldn't be noticing because he worked for my brother Jace at Wild Timber Homes. I also worked there, managing the office.

"I just need the file for the Beast project. Jace said you had it here," he said, his voice low, his eyes darting from my face to the phone in my hand.

I nodded and turned to dig through the paperwork on my table.

"Are you even listening to me, Layne?" I realized I was ignoring Teddy's voice in my ear.

"I'm tired of listening to the same thing over and over. I just need you to meet me at the insurance place tomorrow morning so we can get this done."

"We should meet up to talk first."

I took a deep breath, then another, my eyes landing on Elias as they often had since I started managing Wild Timber two months ago.

As I took him in, an idea hit me. Potentially a really stupid one, but if it got me through this breakup, it would be worth it. "I'm seeing someone new, Teddy." I blurted it out before I had the chance to talk myself out of it.

Elias jerked his head in my direction, eyes wide behind his glasses.

I mouthed the word HELP in his direction, then put the phone on speaker.

"I don't believe you," Teddy said.

"It's true. I didn't want to tell you because it's none of your business, but it's true."

Teddy had the nerve to laugh.

Again.

How the hell I had been with this guy for so long without noticing what an absolute tool he was, I had no idea.

"Come on, Layne. I didn't think you'd stoop low enough to lie to me. We both know we're going to work this out. You expect me to believe you found someone to replace me in that shithole town you're pouting in?"

My blood boiled.

He thought I couldn't do better than him?

I opened my mouth, ready to let him have it, but my phone was plucked from my hand.

Elias flashed me a tight smile. "Meet her at the insurance office when she told you to. Better yet, get there early. Don't make me ask twice."

"Who the fuck are you?" I could practically see his trademark sneer.

"I'm the one she upgraded to." He hit the red button to end the call and handed me my phone back.

All I could do was stare.

Elias was an easygoing guy. Funny and sweet. Clearly he had

another side, and it was the sexiest thing I'd ever seen.

"Thanks," I said, my voice coming out breathy. I clenched my thighs together as an ache started to form there. I was glad to be rid of Teddy, but a woman had needs. Needs I was very interested in having Elias fulfill.

He gave me a nod and a little smile. "He's still giving you a hard time, huh? Can't you just block him?"

I laughed, but there was no real humor in it. "I wish. Our lives are still tangled together. I've gotten almost everything separated without having to see him, but I have three things left to do that we both have to be there in person for. We both need to sign for the changes to our car insurance, bank accounts, and the lease on our rental place."

"Once that's done, so is he?"

I nodded. "Unfortunately, he's using my needing to see him as proof to himself that I want him back." I took a deep breath and sank into a chair. "I thought if he knew I was with someone else, he would drop it. But that only works if he buys my story."

He flashed me that grin again. "Then we'll have to really sell it."

Chapter Two

Elias

What the hell am I doing?

I mentally berated myself as I walked from Layne's front door to my truck. It was snowing lightly, typical of late November, and my boots crunched over the layer that had already accumulated.

This was a terrible idea.

Layne was just getting out of a messy almost-marriage. She was also my co-worker and my boss's sister.

Doing her a favor would be one thing. But I'd had a schoolyard crush on her since the first time she came by the shop to see Jace and it had only gotten worse since she started working there.

I was playing with fire, and for someone who worked with timber, that was dangerous.

I could tell myself that stepping in on her phone call was just to help her out. In reality, I was thinking partly with my heart and partly with my dick.

Jace had told me all about what an ass her ex is. Two seconds of hearing him talk confirmed it. I wanted Layne to be free of him, for her sake and hell, maybe for mine, too.

I tossed the paperwork onto the passenger seat of my truck and started the ignition. The big diesel rumbled to life, and I carefully backed down the long winding driveway that led to Layne's cabin.

I stopped off at Bend's Best Brew and grabbed a twelve-pack of donuts to take to the office before driving to work. I should have gotten these first and given one to Layne. Sounds like she could use some sprinkles in her morning.

I pulled into the yard of Wild Timber Homes ten minutes later, my truck bouncing over the ruts in the road, unseen under the snow. I went straight into the office, where Jace was sitting behind Layne's computer, frowning at the screen.

"Why do you let her work from home one day a week when you can't figure out how to use a computer?" I asked, stomping the snow off my boots. Jace glanced up from the screen.

"Because she's my sister, and she needs a day away from you animals."

He was kidding, but a pit formed in my stomach anyway. Jace was protective of his sister, but not in a pushy way. He had accepted her decision to marry Teddy even though he didn't get along with the guy. Trusting her to know what she wanted. I wondered if he would still accept her decisions when she met someone new.

If he knew what I had just done or what ran through my head when I did it, he would definitely have something to say about it.

I held out the box of donuts and Jace poked his nose over the side and took a chocolate one.

"Here's the file for the Beast project. I just stopped by Layne's and grabbed it."

"Oh, good." Jace took it from my hand, then gave me an inquisitive look. "She okay?"

I plunked down in the chair across from his desk. There was no point in lying about what had happened.

"When I got there, she was on the phone with Teddy. He was giving her a hard time."

Jace sat up straighter in his chair and I could see the muscles in his jaw working. Like me, he was wearing jeans and a dusty flannel. "What did he want now?"

"Trying to get her to meet up to talk. Figures, they can work it out."

He frowned. "He thinks he has a better chance of taking over dad's company when he retires if he's married to Layne. That's his motivation for all this."

"Well, she has a strategy to get rid of him." I took a deep breath. "She said she was seeing someone new. Just to get him to back off, you know?" I added quickly. "When he didn't believe her, I took the phone and talked to him, pretending to be the guy."

Jace's eyebrows went up so high they disappeared under his ball cap. "What?"

I nodded, trying to keep the heat out of my cheeks. "Yeah. Her plan only works if he believes her, so I tried to help." I resisted the urge to squirm as he studied me.

Jace clicked his tongue against his teeth. "Good. Thanks, then. Whatever gets that fuckhead out of her life."

He went back to eating his donut, and I relaxed my shoulders. "No problem."

Except it was a problem.

A big one.

Maybe talking on the phone was all she would need from me, but I had a feeling there would be more to it. And the more time I spent with her, the harder it would be to ignore my crush.

I needed to distract myself with some work, and luckily there was plenty to do even in the winter.

Wild Timber Homes made custom log homes on site here. We built them, then took them apart, shipped the parts where they needed to go and put them back together on location. It was controlled chaos, and usually I liked that.

Wyatt, the only one capable of running the software we used to design the projects, came through the door a moment later. His shaggy dark hair was half hidden under a toque and he was wearing his trademark grin, the kind that usually meant trouble for someone else. "Hey Bossman, hey E, ooh donuts, score." He grabbed one from the box and shoved half of it into his mouth.

"Why so quiet in here?" he asked around a mouthful of baked goodness. "You break the computer again, Jace?"

Jace frowned, folding his arms over his chest. "No. I'm about to throw this demon box out the window though."

Wyatt's grin widened. "Violence already? It's not even lunch."

"This stupid thing has no mercy."

"More changes to the Beast, I assume?" Wyatt asked, tossing his hat and jacket aside.

Jace nodded and moved so Wyatt could do his thing, muttering something under his breath that sounded like a death threat to our software.

Wild Timber Homes had been contracted to build a massive lodge for a resort in Banff. Three levels, seventy rooms and enough custom details to make any sane builder pause. We'd affectionately nicknamed the project the Beast. They wanted carvings and rockwork, wraparound decks, exposed beams.

None of it was outside our skill set. The problem was the client Marin, who kept changing her damned mind.

"I'll be in the yard if you need me," I said, craving the distraction. We may not know the exact final measurements for the entire project, but I could still start picking logs to be prepped.

As I examined the lumber we had on hand, my mind wandered back to Layne. Her life with Teddy had been very different. But over the last two months it had been so clear she fit in here. She was sharp and kind and put up with a bunch of messy lumberjacks without complaint.

I just hoped once she had Teddy in the rearview mirror, she wouldn't put Wild Timber Homes and me in the same place.

I pushed the thoughts from my head.

I knew she would be meeting Teddy at the insurance office. I even knew when.

What I didn't know was whether I should be there.

My head said no.

This was none of my business. Besides, Layne was capable and independent. She could deal with him on her own, and if she wanted help, she would ask for it.

The problem was my instinct said I should be. That Teddy would use my absence as proof that the boyfriend Layne claimed to have didn't exist.

I told myself I wouldn't go.

Even as my mind was already counting the minutes until morning.

Chapter Three

Layne

I glanced at the time on my phone for the hundredth time.

7:42 a.m.

Way too early to be sitting outside the insurance office. It didn't open until eight, but once I'd woken up that morning, I hadn't been able to sit still. I needed to get this done. To have it go smoothly. And, more importantly, I needed to focus on getting my life in order and not on Elias.

Maybe it was just how different he was from Teddy that had him in my head. Teddy had a main character syndrome that I hadn't recognized at first. He had to be the center of attention, the life of the party. Dressing and acting in a way to make sure everyone around him knew he had money in the bank and influence when it was needed.

I knew he had plans to climb the ladder at Dad's company, and I'd always suspected part of the reason he dated me was to help with that goal.

Elias, on the other hand, was a calm, steady, hardworking guy.

I had debated asking him to come with me today, but had dismissed the idea. Having the ex meet the pretend new boyfriend was a terrible idea. There was no need for drama or even conversation. We just needed to explain the situation to the clerk, sign on the dotted line, and go our separate ways.

What if Teddy took Elias's absence as proof I was lying, though?

I worried my lower lip.

I had already shut the engine off, causing the cold to seep into the car, creeping up from the floorboards, and toward my feet.

Dammit, maybe I should call Elias.

I stared at my phone in my lap, my thumb hovering over his name. I didn't want to bother him. He worked hard. Everyone at Wild Timber did.

He'd shown up the day I moved into my cabin. He hadn't commented on my red-rimmed eyes, or knotted hair. He'd just moved boxes and left me his cell number in case I needed anything.

At 7:46, there was a knock on my window. I looked up, expecting to see Teddy, but instead Elias stood outside my car as if I had summoned him. He had a drink tray in his hands and a sheepish look on his face.

I pushed the door open and got out. "Hey, what are you doing here?"

"I was grabbing a coffee and figured you might need one." He held out the drink tray.

"Thanks, I could definitely use one." I took the cup closest to me. It instantly warmed my hands. I took a sip, and it was the perfect level of sweet. The fact that he knew my coffee order didn't surprise me.

He paid attention.

"So this was all a coincidence then?" I teased.

He rubbed the back of his neck. The movement, combined with his glasses, made him look like anything but the capable mountain man I knew him to be. "I wasn't sure if you wanted me to be here for this or not. Seemed like that Teddy guy's never been told no. I can go before he gets here, but I just thought I'd offer." His breath was visible in the air between us.

A smile crept over my mouth. "You could have just texted, E."

A blush crept up his neck and into his cheeks. "I know. I just don't have much patience for cell phones."

His excuse was thin at best, but I was happy to see him all the same. The tight knot in my chest eased a little, replaced by something warmer, and far more dangerous.

I wondered if Jace had sent him, and my happiness faltered. It was a scenario that made sense.

My brother trusted me, but he was protective. He and Teddy had been like oil and water, but I'd written off their exchanges as good-natured fun.

It bothered me now how easily I'd dismissed Teddy's teasing. How many times I'd laughed when I shouldn't have.

At least something good had come out of it. Sloane and Jace had fallen in love somewhere between picking out a tux and setting up for the reception.

Jace was happier than I'd ever seen him.

"I appreciate it, but I'm good."

"I told Jace about what I said to Teddy on the phone, just figured it was better he knew in case Teddy came by work or something."

I nodded. So my suspicion about Jace's hand in this was probably right. "Good thinking."

"You sure you're okay?" He slouched just enough to look into my eyes through his glasses.

"Yeah, thanks, I'm good."

He nodded, took a half step back, then nodded again. "I'll see you at the office, then."

There was something unspoken in his eyes, a question he didn't ask. That he respected my choice after months of Teddy's dismissive bullshit made me like him that much more.

That his helpfulness could in part be my brother's doing made me remember to keep my heart guarded.

I gave him a small wave and watched him go, his long legs eating up the sidewalk. After a minute, I turned to get back into my car and out of the cold, but I almost ran right into Teddy.

"Shit, you scared me."

He rolled his eyes. "You demanded I show up, so here I am." He hunched his shoulders against the cold. "Is that the upgrade?" He made air quotes around the word *upgrade*. "Another lumberjack? Jesus, Layne. When you rebel, you commit."

Teddy had always looked down on Jace for his job, seeing trades as mindless and beneath him.

I grit my teeth, refusing to take the bait. "Let's just get this over with." I would have loved to verbally bitch-slap him, but I needed his signature more than I needed the satisfaction.

He made a grand gesture for me to go first, and I stormed up the stairs.

We emerged twenty minutes later with everything done.

I was shocked at how smoothly it had gone.

Was Teddy trying to butter me up, or had he finally accepted this was over?

"We should come up with a day and time to meet at the bank,

get the accounts dealt with."

"Whatever you say, *dear,*" Teddy said, sliding his hands into expensive-looking leather gloves.

I ignored the passive-aggressive dig and got into my car. "I'll text you," I said before slamming the door with a satisfying thud.

I couldn't get away from Teddy fast enough.

Chapter Four

Elias

So she didn't want me to stay. No big deal. I hadn't expected her to. It was fine.

I had a shit ton of work to do anyway.

I arrived at work and stepped into the office to find Zane and Wyatt already there. The place smelled like coffee and sawdust, which meant they'd both been up early too. "Ready for another day working on the Beast?" I asked as I put my lunch away.

"I updated the plans, again," Wyatt said, stretching his back from behind a computer in the office, bones cracking like he was twice his age. "So if you want to actually run a chainsaw today, you can get started."

"A minor miracle," Zane added, flipping through the pages. "I told Marin, no more changes."

I raised an eyebrow. "Since when are you the one talking to clients? Isn't that Layne's job?" Of all the boisterous guys who worked here, Zane was the quietest.

A bit of color crept into his cheeks. "We all do our part." He studied the pages before him like they might rescue him from the conversation, so I let it go.

Wyatt wrapped his arm around Zane's neck and ruffled his hair. "The ghost over here actually talked to a person. Mark it on the calendar."

Zane batted him away and gave him the finger, expression otherwise unchanged.

Jace came into the office and raised an eyebrow, taking in the scene in one sweep. "Do I have to separate you two?"

"No, *Dad*," Wyatt said with a laugh.

Layne poked her nose around the corner of her computer screen. "Never call him that. It's just weird."

Wyatt's grin grew wider. "How about *Daddy* then?"

Layne made a retching sound. "Get out of my office, all of you."

Wyatt definitely said *yes Mom* under his breath as he collected his coat. Either Layne didn't hear him, or didn't take the bait.

I grabbed a chainsaw, a measuring tape, and a list of measurements and headed out into the yard, feeling the need to move. I craved that bone-deep physical exhaustion that only this job could provide.

It was cold and bright out, and snow crunched under my boots, and I headed out to select the perfect log for this portion of the project.

The job was fifty percent science, fifty percent art, and one hundred percent dangerous. Logs weighing several thousand pounds, power tools, heavy equipment, dust, noise, and stress from clients who couldn't make up their goddamned minds were all part of the equation.

For that reason, I needed to focus on the task at hand, and

not on Layne.

By lunchtime, I was more sawdust than a man. The muscles in my forearms and thighs ached, my shoulders burned, and my shirt stuck to my skin with sweat despite the cold weather. The air tasted like pine sap and chainsaw exhaust, the kind of smell that usually grounded me. I'd made some headway on the project, assuming nothing had changed.

I hadn't seen Zane, Wyatt, or Jace in a while. Hopefully that didn't mean they were in the office redesigning. More likely, they were in another part of the yard working out some finer details.

I made my way back to the office for lunch and coffee. So much coffee.

"Stop!" Layne yelled as I opened the door, but before I could actually step through it.

I froze. "What?"

She stood up from her desk, hands on her hips. "You can't come in here like that. You'll make a mess."

"I need someone to blow me off, and there was no one else in the yard."

Her face turned an interesting shade of scarlet, and I was pretty sure mine did too once I realized what I'd said. "The compressed air, I mean."

She licked her lips, fighting back a laugh. "Go outside. I'll help you."

I walked back out to the shop, my heart thumping faster than it had any right to. The cold bit at my damp skin, raising goosebumps along my arms, but I barely noticed. All my attention was locked on her. Layne followed, then grabbed the air compressor hose and turned it on, sending a powerful blast of air at me. Dust exploded off my clothes and into the air.

I pressed my lips together and squeezed my eyes shut.

"God, Elias, you are a mess," she called over the sound of the compressor. "Turn around so I can get your back."

I could hear Layne giggling as she worked, the sound light and unguarded. It threaded straight through me, settling low in my gut and making it hard to breathe. I focused on the way the air hit me, dust trying to get up my nose, anything to drive the image of her standing so close out of my head.

Finally, she shut it off and set the hose aside. We were standing closer together than was strictly necessary. Close enough that I could smell her shampoo, something clean and faintly floral that didn't belong out here among sawdust and diesel.

"Am I clean enough to come into your office now, Your Highness?" I did a slow turn for her inspection.

She reached out and swiped her hand over my shoulder, dislodging a few stubborn flecks of wood. "It'll do."

Her fingers lingered for half a second too long, and the casual touch landed like a spark. I blinked the dust from my eyes and took her in. Her blonde hair was pulled back from her face, her curvy figure tucked into a well-fitting pair of slacks and a blouse. Some of the dust from me had settled on her. She was a combination of perfectly put-together and a little chaotic.

On the surface, she belonged to a different world than mine, one with polished desks and spreadsheets, but somehow she stood here in the snow and sawdust, fitting in just fine. Her eyes sparkled with amusement, and I loved the way she looked when she laughed.

"Thanks," I said, swallowing hard, trying to keep my eyes from drifting to her mouth. This had to be the most inconvenient crush I'd ever had.

She smirked, brushing some of the sawdust from her blouse.

"You're lucky I'm feeling generous today." She shivered.

I was hot from work, but she was outside in the snow without a coat.

"Let's head back then." We walked back to the office, and I pushed the door open and held it, letting her slip past me, her shoulder grazing the center of my chest. She stood stomping the snow off her shoes, and I took my boots right off; they were a lost cause.

We were standing close, and I fought the urge to lean in closer. I had to keep perspective. "So… how'd it go with Teddy?" I didn't even like saying his name, and the thought of her with him splashed cold water on the feelings bubbling below the surface.

The amusement drained from her face. "Surprisingly smooth. We got done what needed to be done. The fact that he didn't put up a fuss seems more suspicious than good."

"I can come with you to the next meetup," I said too quickly.

She cocked her head to the side. "For moral support, or…?"

I nodded. "Really sell the fake story, you know?"

She nodded too, her gaze flicking down my chest once before meeting my eyes again. The look made my pulse jump, and I scolded myself. Not sure if I was seeing things I wanted to see or if that appreciative look in her eye was really there. "I might just take you up on that. Then again, if I don't, will you just happen to be in the area again?" she teased.

Heat crept up my neck. I was certain I hadn't blushed this much in my entire life. "I do go to the bank from time to time. I could coincidentally show up at the same time as you."

She took a half-step closer. "Then I'll let you know when. Just in case."

The door opened behind us, and we jumped apart. "Oh good,

Layne, can you print the updated bill for the Henderson place? I changed a few things on the spreadsheet last night. Hey, Elias."

"You touched the spreadsheet? Jace, leave these things for me," Layne snapped as she stormed behind her desk.

"I think I'm in trouble," Jace muttered.

As I watched Layne's curvy frame march towards her desk, my skin still buzzing where she'd stood close beside me, I thought I might be in trouble too.

Chapter Five

Layne

R*ound two, here we go.*

My mood was sour as I pulled up in front of the bank. The parking lot was tiny, and I nosed my car into a spot that was maybe a little too small. I didn't plan to be there more than ten minutes anyway.

That was assuming Teddy was in as agreeable a mood as he'd been last time.

I got out of the car, careful not to bang my door into the one next to me, and stood on the sidewalk watching the road for Teddy. I stepped from foot to foot to keep warm. It was a clear day, blue sky overhead, but those were often the coldest.

As I glanced around, I couldn't help but notice a Wild Timber truck parallel parked on the street half a block back.

Elias.

It had to be.

The thought brought a smile to my face.

I had never been one for old fairy tales where the princess was helpless and saved by the knight. But having him offer to help, then give me space to handle things myself, was working for me in a way I really didn't need right now.

A few minutes later, Teddy's car showed up. He circled the lot before finding a spot, then stalked his way over to me.

"What, no lumberjack protection today?"

I frowned. "Let's just get this done."

He made no move toward the building. "Layne, before I sign another thing, we need to talk about us."

Fucking hell, not this again.

"No, we don't."

"Because you have a new boyfriend, right?" he sneered.

I huffed out a breath. It was visible in the cold air between us. "No, because I'm telling you I don't want to be with you anymore. The fact that I'm with someone else is none of your business."

He crossed his arms over his chest, his expensive coat pulled tight at the shoulders. "It does, actually. I figured this whole thing out."

I raised my eyebrows. "Then enlighten me."

"You were pissed that I didn't sing your brother's praises for setting up a few chairs at our wedding. So now you're pretending to date someone like him to get my attention."

Jace had done more than set up chairs. He had set up the entire reception, and made me a custom arbor. Teddy had dismissed the whole thing as brainless work, and that had been the moment I'd finally seen him clearly.

"I don't want your attention," I said. "I want your signature."

"I notice you didn't deny the fact that the boyfriend is fake."

I rubbed my temples.

How can I even argue with something this arrogant?

Teddy stepped closer and put his hands on my shoulders. I tried to step back, but he held firm. "Come on, Layne. This has gone on long enough. It's time to come home."

I was debating if it was worth it to kick Teddy in the groin when I heard footsteps in heavy boots on the sidewalk, coming fast. I looked up to see Elias heading toward us. Teddy still had his hands on my shoulders, and I half expected Elias to punch him out, based on the intensity of his gaze.

That would only make things worse.

Teddy was exactly the type to press charges and make someone's life miserable.

Elias had something else up his sleeve.

"Hey babe, how are you?" Elias asked with a smile as he approached.

He reached out, but instead of knocking Teddy on his ass, he stepped between us, forcing Teddy to let go. His eyes held mine as he wrapped his arms around my waist, pulling me flush against his solid chest.

Instinctively, I wrapped my arms around his neck, feeling the short hair at the nape and sliding my fingers through it.

He pulled me against his chest and enveloped me in the familiar, comforting smell of pine. The cold that had been stinging my cheeks was a distant annoyance, all but forgotten as I focused on how good it felt to be wrapped in his arms.

"Everything okay?" he murmured, his breath skating over the skin of my neck.

I nodded. "Thank you for coming, anyway."

I was a lot shorter than he was; my eyes usually level with his nipples, so I rose onto my toes to press myself closer, burying my cold nose in his neck.

Chapter Five

His stubble scraped my cheek, something I'd never experienced with baby-faced Teddy. I wouldn't have guessed it, but the roughness sent a thrill down my spine, and I shivered in his arms. He pulled me closer, his hands sliding an inch or two lower on my waist. I mentally encouraged him to go lower, wondering what his firm grip would feel like on my ass.

There was a strange sense of safety in his arms. A permission to let go, or just be. Unfortunately, life butted its way back in.

"You've made your point, Layne."

Teddy's voice cut through my happy little bubble, and I reluctantly let my arms fall from Elias's shoulders. Even then, I didn't look away. I couldn't. His eyes locked on mine, his cheeks flushed. His expression was a mix of concern, and arousal.

Fuck. I wish we were alone.

He mouthed, *you okay*, and I nodded again.

"How rude of me not to introduce myself. I'm Elias." He held his hand out to Teddy, who wrinkled his nose as if he'd been offered a dead fish. A long beat passed before Elias shrugged and slipped his hand into his pocket.

"I'll wait for you guys to be done. We can carpool to the office," he said, one arm settling possessively around my waist.

"She brought her own car," Teddy snarked.

Elias shrugged. "Well then, we can drive back together. Convoy style. Do what you have to do. I'll wait for you here."

Reluctantly, I let his arm fall from around my waist. Teddy and I started toward the bank.

Heat flushed my cheeks. I could still feel the ghost of Elias's touch on my skin.

I knew I'd be thinking about his touch later, when I was alone and under the covers. For now, I had something I needed to do.

It was clear Teddy had more to say, but he wasn't willing to try with Elias there. I wasn't sure why he could be an ass to my brother but seemed intimidated by Elias, but I liked it.

I liked it a lot.

Chapter Six

Elias

My workday passed in a haze. I couldn't even say for sure if I'd actually been at work. I had no idea what I did or who I talked to.

What did I have for lunch?

No clue.

What color shirt did I have on?

Couldn't tell you.

All I thought about was how right it had felt to pull Layne to my chest and hold her there.

Sure, it had been satisfying to see Teddy standing there like an ass while I had my hands on Layne. But it was a footnote if that. The main story was her fingers carding through my hair, her body pressed tightly against mine, my jacket smelling like her perfume. She hadn't seemed any more eager to step away than I had.

The whole moment had my hopes up and excitement flooding

through my system.

"Don't forget, dinner at my place tonight," Jace said as I gathered my things at the end of the day.

Oh, fuck, I had forgotten.

Not that I didn't like spending extra time with everyone, but I'd had important plans to go home and jerk off. Now I'd have to run home, shower and get to Jace's place before the animals I worked with ate all the food. "I'll be there."

These Friday night get-togethers were fairly new. Jace had always been a head-down workaholic. When he got together with Sloane a few months ago, that had changed. He still worked damn hard, especially when she was away for work. But when she was home, he wanted to celebrate, and when she was gone, he wanted distraction.

Sloane had suggested having everyone from Wild Timber over every Friday night, and Jace had run with it. It was a nice gesture by my boss, which just made me feel guilty for how I'd held his sister in my arms.

Jace headed out the door, giving me a glimpse of the snow as it piled up in the yard. It had been coming down hard all day.

I turned to look at Layne, who was working quietly behind her computer. "Do you want me to pick you up for dinner at Jace's place tonight?"

She raised a brow. "I can drive myself, you know?"

I fumbled for an excuse. "I know. There's just a lot of snow today, and your car…the ground clearance is low compared to my truck."

She pushed back from her desk, her chair rolling across the floor. "That's true. Sure, thanks. Pick me up at six?"

I nodded, feeling like I'd just asked my crush to prom and she'd said yes.

Chapter Six

I headed out to my truck, brushed the snow off the hood, windshield and roof, then climbed inside and started the engine. My hands were already half numb, but I didn't care. I wrapped my fingers around the cold steering wheel and drove home to get ready for the night.

Step one was a shower.

I was chilled from a full day of working outside; the mix of snow and sweat and more snow having a way of doing that. I shed my clothes, aware I was leaving a trail of sawdust through the house that I'd have to clean up later. Once the water warmed, I stepped under the spray and sighed at how good it felt.

It had been a demanding day, and I was more interested in sleep than going to Jace's place. We were making some headway on the Beast project. A lot of the basic structure pieces were ready to go now. It was frustrating since we would make progress then either have a delay in materials or the client would change her mind.

That could all wait though; tonight, I could spend some time with Layne.

The thought of her had my cock stirring as I rubbed soap over my skin. I remembered the feel of her pressed against my chest. Her sweet scent, the things we could have done if we'd been alone.

We could have ditched all our winter layers and felt her body against mine. I could have captured those tempting lips, left her with beard burn on her neck. I pictured ripping her blouse open and teasing her ample breasts with my hands or my mouth.

I slid my hand down my stomach, washing my skin and teasing myself at the same time, before taking my cock in hand and giving it a slow stroke. "Shit." I braced one hand against the shower wall.

In my mind, Layne was unbuttoning my jeans and freeing my cock. It was her hand wrapped around me, not my own. I'd do the same to her, strip her down, then hike one of her tempting thighs up over my hip. Maybe I'd tease her clit for a while, watch her eyes roll back and her breath catch. Maybe I'd just sink into her and we'd both groan, then slam into each other hard, over and over.

The images of bare skin and teasing touches flooded my mind. I jerked myself faster, knowing I shouldn't be thinking about my boss's sister, but beyond caring.

I wanted her; I couldn't deny it.

I wanted all that organized, strong-minded energy of hers focused on me in the best possible way.

Groaning, I picked up speed, my hand flying over me with single-minded focus. The water slid over my sensitive skin, but in my mind it was all her.

Her touch, her breath, her hair.

My balls drew tight against my body, and I painted the shower wall with my release. I scrambled for balance against the slick tile of my shower, my legs shaking as everything I had poured out of me.

I stood there naked and dripping, fighting to catch my breath, surprised by the power of my orgasm.

It wasn't like I hadn't gotten off in a long time. But there was something about Layne that just did it for me, and that was a problem.

A problem that would be hard to hide at Jace's place tonight.

Chapter Seven

Layne

The drive from my place to Jace's was less than ten minutes. Even so, the idea of that extra time alone with Elias had me pacing my living room.

It was too soon for me to be interested in a new man.

That he was my pretend boyfriend and was treating me better than the man I'd actually been engaged to was messing with my head.

I needed to focus on the task at hand: get rid of Teddy from every aspect of my life.

After that, maybe I could think about other things, but for now I had to stay focused. Elias was kindly helping me meet my goal. I couldn't afford to confuse that with anything more than friendship.

God knew I'd made enough mistakes with men to last me a lifetime.

Maybe an evening with my friends and co-workers would

distract me from what was going on and I could keep Elias in the right place in my brain. A group setting would remind me how things worked. He was my brother's employee and friend. He was now my co-worker and friend too.

Nothing more.

Even if it felt fantastic to be in his arms.

I hated to arrive empty-handed, even though Jace said he had everything handled, so I put together a quick plate of meat and cheese and wrapped it up just in time to see headlights illuminating my driveway. Snow was still falling, those light flakes the size of golf balls that looked beautiful but accumulated quickly.

I was no stranger to driving in snow, but it was nice to let someone else worry about it. Especially because this way I could have a few glasses of wine.

Although lowering my inhibitions tonight might not be the best idea.

I stepped out the front door and locked it behind me, the cold biting at my ears.

I crossed the driveway, snow crunching under my boots, and climbed into Elias's truck. There was a bakery bag on the seat between us, so clearly I wasn't the only one who hated to arrive empty-handed.

"Hey," I said, buckling my seat belt.

The truck smelled like freshly cut wood, but underneath that was what could only be his body wash or deodorant. Something spicy and masculine that made me want to shift a little closer.

Which was bad.

I had literally just pep-talked this crush out of my head and now it was back because he smelled good.

Ugh. How low is the bar?

"Hey yourself, ready for this?"

I nodded. "I'm starving."

"Yeah, me too." He backed smoothly out of my driveway and onto the road. "Has Jace said anything to you about our whole fake dating thing?"

I shook my head. "Been too busy with the Beast. I think it slipped his mind. Why?"

"No reason." He gave a shrug that almost passed for nonchalance. "Just curious if the guys are going to give us the third degree."

I hadn't thought of that. Teasing was fine, but it would be hard to take when the underlying feelings were developing. "We can handle it."

He nodded and focused on the road.

I studied him in the dim light for a moment before turning away. Staring at him was doing nothing for my crush.

The drive was mercifully short, and when we arrived, I could see a line of Wild Timber trucks and my best friend Sloane's car.

We were still working on getting back to our old rhythm after things had been strained while I stressed about my wedding and she quietly fell for my brother.

She was enjoying a new relationship while I was mourning the end of an old one.

Maybe tonight could be normal. Focus on time with my best friend instead of whatever weirdness I was feeling toward Elias.

We walked in the front door, and Sloane met us with a smile. "You guys made it, man it is really coming down out there, eh?"

"Sure is." We all headed into the kitchen, and I put the platter I'd brought on the counter. Sloane snatched the bakery bag from Elias. "Are these the little cupcakes you brought last time?

Oh, I could kiss you."

He laughed. "I'm not dumb enough to show up without them. Where are the guys?"

"Out back," Sloane said, already helping herself to a cupcake.

Elias grabbed a beer and headed out the door.

I cocked an eyebrow. "Why are they outside?"

She shrugged as she chewed. "Jace insisted on barbecuing even though it's below zero and dumping snow."

I laughed. "Sounds like my brother."

She nodded. She was clearly gone over the guy. I hadn't known until after they got together that they'd both been crushing on each other since we were teenagers.

"Wine?"

I snorted. "As if you have to ask."

She frowned. "Is it not going well with Teddy?"

She poured us each a glass, and we settled onto the sofa. I filled her in on how things had been going with separating Teddy's life from mine.

"Hold on, so Elias has been pretending to be your boyfriend?" She nudged my shoulder with hers.

My cheeks heated, and I told myself it was the glass of red that was already half gone.

"It's not as exciting as it sounds. He literally just talked to Teddy on the phone and showed up when we met."

"Did you want him to do more?" She wiggled her eyebrows.

I giggled. "We're co-workers. He's my brother's employee. There can be no more."

Sloane pulled her legs up under her on the couch. She wore leggings and a slouchy sweatshirt, looking casual and comfortable in the home she shared with my brother. A stark contrast to the high-powered lawyer she was at her job.

"Look, I can't talk about my sex life since it involves your brother."

"Eww. Mental block."

She rolled her eyes. "I'm just saying, you don't have to take a vow of celibacy just because Teddy didn't turn out to be the one. Elias is cute, and he wouldn't have jumped at the chance to be your fake boyfriend if he didn't think of you that way."

I glanced over my shoulder toward the window. The guys were standing out on the deck, drinking cold beer despite the frigid temperature. My gaze found Elias easily; the light catching on his glasses.

He was exactly the kind of person Teddy loved to demean. Blue collar. Made his living with his hands. Honest, hardworking, not scheming or manipulative. Just doing what needed to be done.

I'd be lying if I said I hadn't watched him on the job site more than I should have. He was hot. Sloane wasn't wrong.

"He's a helpful guy; I don't think it's any deeper than that."

"You don't have to punish yourself for Teddy's sins forever," Sloane said, refilling my glass from the bottle. "Just think about it."

Little did she know that was all I had been thinking about.

Chapter Eight

Elias

Jace looked over his shoulder through the window into the house, then back at me. "How's this shit with Teddy going? I didn't want to ask Layne in case it upset her."

I snorted. "You don't know your sister very well if you're worried about that. If you haven't been called to post bail, she's fine."

He laughed. "Okay, fair. Just tell me if something happens, alright?" He flipped a burger on the grill. It was fucking freezing out, but we were all used to it. Cold that made your lungs sting was just part of being Canadian.

"Why would you know what's going on with Layne?" Zane asked, taking a long pull from his beer. He was a quiet guy by nature, but a beer or two into the conversation he loosened up.

Jace closed the barbecue lid, cutting off some of the heat that had been soaking into us. "Elias, did you not share with the class?"

Chapter Eight

Wyatt and Zane looked between the two of us. "Don't tell me you're banging the bossman's sister," Wyatt said with a laugh.

Jace shot him a death glare. "No one is banging anyone. Well, except me and my super-hot lawyer girlfriend. But Layne's in a shitty spot, trying to get rid of Teddy."

"I'm acting as a fake boyfriend so Teddy gets the idea and backs off," I said, feeling my cheeks heat and hoping the darkness around us covered it.

Wyatt eyed the two of us. A smile slowly spreading over his lips. "No way. This is too good."

"It's not a big deal," I insisted, trying not to sound defensive and failing epically.

Wyatt rubbed his hands together. "Must be one hell of a dry spell you're having if you agreed to pretend to date. That's half a step past the Friend Zone."

"Not all of us think with our dicks," I said, wishing he would drop it.

"No, you have the poor bastard muzzled." He leaned down so he was at eye level with my crotch. "Help, I can't breathe in here," he said in a fake cartoon voice.

"Alright, and Wyatt's cut off," Zane said, taking the beer from his hand and dumping the last of it over the railing into the snow.

"Hey!"

Zane shrugged. "Talking dicks is where I draw the line."

"Damn right," Jace said, pointing the neck of his beer bottle at Wyatt.

"Let's see what Layne has to say about that," Wyatt said, already heading for the door into the house.

Wyatt loved to stir up trouble, and he was damned good at it. I turned and followed him inside. My chest feeling tight.

The warmth of the house hit me, and I shivered at the change in temperature. Wyatt had already pulled off his boots and was in the living room where Sloane and Layne were drinking wine on the couch.

"So," he said, a shit-eating grin spreading across his face, "anything new in your world, Layne?"

Layne's eyes darted to me, then back to him. "What are you so happy about?"

He laughed. "I just learned about you and Elias's little arrangement."

She snorted. "You make it sound like some mafia deal."

"Did she make you an offer you couldn't refuse?" Wyatt said, laying the accent on way too thick.

The funny thing was, she had. Or at least she'd presented the opportunity. I wasn't a seize-the-day kind of guy, but when it came to Layne, it was different.

"Something like that," I mumbled.

Wyatt perched on the edge of the couch next to Layne and Sloane. "So let me get this straight. You needed to make your ex jealous, so you picked the human equivalent of a level to get the job done?"

"I—" she started, but of course Wyatt wasn't done.

"A man with the personality of Stonehenge and the dating history of a reclusive monk."

Layne flashed me a sympathetic smile. It did something in my chest.

"Not to mention that I, easily the best-looking of the bunch, was right there as an option."

Layne ran his eyes over him and shrugged. "Meh, you're not my type."

I snorted.

He rubbed the center of his chest. "Damn, you don't pull punches, do you? So, what? Your type is celibate lumberjack nerds?" He jabbed his thumb at me over his shoulder. I adjusted my glasses, and frowned at him.

Sloane put a hand on Wyatt's shoulder. "Elias is the best out of all of you with a chainsaw. You may want to be a little nicer."

Wyatt moved to stand beside me and elbowed me in the ribs. "He knows I'm joking. Makes sense you'd pick Mr. Dependable."

Layne laughed. "Elias is just being a good friend and—"

Her phone vibrated on the table, and the smile slid from her lips. The name *TEDDY* flashed across the screen.

I grabbed the phone off the table. I saw red as I hit the green circle to answer. "What?" I barked.

There was silence for a moment. "I need Layne."

Jace came through the door with a plate piled high with burgers, his brow dropping when he took in the scene.

"Well, you're not getting her. What do you want?"

Teddy snorted. "Fine. Get yourself a piece of paper and a crayon and write this down."

I clenched my jaw.

"I have something for Layne. I'm coming to her house tonight to drop it off. Got it, or do you need me to go slower?"

I glanced at Layne and took a breath. She needed this to stay civil, no matter what kind of shithead he was. So instead of tearing into him, I hung up.

"He's coming to my house?" Layne asked, looking deflated.

I nodded.

She let out a string of curses.

Wyatt clapped a few times, then playfully punched my shoulder. "I take back everything I said. That was impressive. You legit added a growl in there."

I gave a small bow, trying to play it off as nothing, when really I was fuming at Teddy, and watching Layne like a hawk.

Sloane put an arm around her friend. "Let's eat. You'll feel better. Besides, your *boyfriend* will be with you when you get home, right? You guys drove here together?"

She gave me a look that said she knew exactly what was running through my mind. I schooled my features and gave nothing away.

"Carpooling?" Wyatt said. "That's like third base to this guy. Right after eye contact and connecting to the same Wi-Fi signal."

Layne smacked him on the arm and gestured toward the table. "Get some food in to you. Beer makes you an ass."

"He's always an ass," Zane said. "Beer just makes him louder."

We all settled around the table and started passing plates. I sat close to Layne, feeling protective even though I knew that if it came down to it, Teddy wouldn't stand a chance against her.

Wanting to protect her didn't mean I thought she was incapable. I just wanted to do things for her. Make her life easier. Surprise her with coffee. Shovel her driveway. Show up without being asked. Simple shit. The kind that mattered more than swiping a credit card.

I shook the thought from my head. I was in deeper than I wanted to admit.

Dinner passed with the usual joking. The food was great, but I was counting down the minutes until we could leave. Whatever Teddy thought he was doing, it wasn't going to end the way he wanted.

Finally, we all started moving towards the door. Jace grabbed my elbow and guided me a few feet away. "Keep an eye on this Teddy shit, will you?"

I nodded as I shrugged on my jacket. "You think he's violent?"

The corner of his mouth ticked up. "If either of them is, it's definitely her. No, I just don't trust that guy. The less time he spends around my sister, the better."

I nodded. He trusted me around Layne; if he knew what I was thinking about her, he might not.

Chapter Nine

Layne

"Tire tracks. Only one set though," Elias said as he pulled into my driveway. He slowed to a stop and looked at me. It had been snowing non-stop since he picked me up a few hours earlier, so those tracks weren't his. Great, that could only mean one thing. "What do you want to do? Doesn't look like he left."

I chewed my lip. I knew Elias would take me somewhere else if I asked, but I didn't want to hide from Teddy. "Are you okay with sticking with the whole fake-dating thing? I'd rather see what he wants than run away."

He nodded. "Let's do it." The truck started rolling again and once he rounded the bend in the driveway, his headlights illuminated Teddy's car. As Elias eased the truck to a stop and put it in park, Teddy got out of the driver's seat and shoved his hands in his pockets. I climbed out of the truck, dropping into the snow and walked over to talk to him.

"What is it you had to give me that couldn't wait?"

His eyes darted over to where Elias was standing near the door of his truck, giving us space to talk, but not going away. "Can we talk about this inside? Cold out, and we need to figure out when we can meet to work out the lease."

I huffed out a breath. It was cold out. I didn't want him in my space, but this was short-term pain, long-term gain. "Fine." I clomped up the front step in my boots and unlocked the front door, then bypassed Teddy and went to Elias. He brought his hands to my upper arms as I approached and rubbed them to keep them warm.

My heart gave a stupid little flutter.

"Everything okay?" He asked, his voice low. I nodded, shifting closer to him.

"Having to give me something was clearly a lie, but we need to talk about when we're meeting next. I'd like to get it over with."

He nodded. "Why don't I come in with you? Make sure he leaves."

I nodded. "Thanks." I reached out and threaded my fingers through his. His hand was comically big, and the roughness of his palm was so different from mine. I pictured what it would feel like to have those calluses on other places of my body and shivered.

"Let's get inside where it's warm."

He led the way up to my front door, gripping my hand. For just a moment, I could pretend that this was real. That he was my man, and we were heading into our cabin after a night with friends. Maybe we would shower together to warm up, or just slip under the covers and he'd hold me tight.

The image slipped away as I stepped through my front door

to find Teddy having made himself comfortable at my kitchen table. Boots and jacket off, leaning back as if he were welcome here. Teddy looked up as we walked through the door, and his eyes narrowed at Elias. "Does he really need to be here for this?"

I ignored him, peeling off my winter layers, then sat at the table opposite Teddy. Elias came to stand behind me, a steady presence at my back. "So, when are you available to get this lease sorted out?"

He ran a hand through his hair. It was a strangely vulnerable thing for him to do; he was notoriously unflappable. He and I compared calendars and came up with a few times we could suggest to the real estate agent. It went strangely smoothly, which should have been my first clue that something was up. "Alright, I will email the real estate agent and we can figure out what works for them," I said.

Teddy nodded and stood, but rather than put on his coat he went to the window in the kitchen and looked out.

"It is really coming down out there. Might be dangerous to drive home."

And there it was.

The ulterior motive I was waiting for.

I stood and crossed my arms over my chest. "I don't have a spare room for you to stay, so you'll have to figure something out." I didn't want anything bad to happen to him, but I wasn't about to open my home to him either.

"Figure something out? Like what?"

"I have a spare room," Elias said, putting an arm around my shoulders. The weight of it was calming, and the subtle smell of pine surrounded me. "We can go to my place in my truck. It does fine in the snow. I'll bring you back in the morning when I come to get Layne for work."

Chapter Nine

Teddy's face was priceless. Like a deer in the headlights, but with more attitude. "I'm not staying at your house."

Elias shrugged and adjusted his glasses. "Alright, well Layne can stay with me and you can stay here then. That okay with you?" he asked, looking down at me.

I beamed at him and nodded.

It was okay.

Maybe too okay.

I wasn't sure how I would sleep in his space and not want to get my hands on all six feet of sexy lumberjack, but I'd have to persevere. I nodded and pressed further into his side.

Teddy pushed back from the table, grabbed his coat, and started for the door. "Forget it, I have snow tires and a credit card. Worst case, I'll get towed home."

Elias kept his arm firmly around my shoulders as we watched Teddy put on his boots and stomp out the door. We stood at the window watching him clear snow from the top of his car. "Should we really drive the point home?" Elias asked, his mouth inches from my ear.

"What did you have in mind?"

"Can I kiss you…just so Teddy knows we're really together?" A flush crept up his cheeks, and my heart thudded in my chest.

I nodded and turned in his arms. I wrapped my hands around the nape of his neck, burying my fingers in the short hair like I had before. I went up on my tiptoes and he hunched to meet me, his lips pressing against mine. His lips felt soft even as his stubble scraped my chin.

I forgot how to breathe.

He wrapped his arms more tightly around my waist, pulling me flush against him. I went willingly, not able to get close enough. I let my hands slide down over his shoulders, feeling the strength of the muscles there. He gasped at the contact, and I slid my tongue between his parted lips. He tasted sweet, like the cupcake's we'd had at Jace's place, and I greedily massaged his tongue with mine. His hands inched lower, his longer fingers splayed over the top of my ass, and either he had something in his pocket or he was as excited as I was.

I heard an engine start in the driveway and reminded myself this was all for show.

I didn't pull back.

Not right away.

I selfishly took one more long moment to enjoy the feel of Elias's body against mine.

Chapter Ten

Elias

It was only when the headlights of Teddy's car cut through the dim cabin that I pulled my lips from hers.

I didn't want to.

My dick really didn't want to.

But this was all for show, and with the ex out of the driveway, there was no reason for me to keep my body pressed against hers.

Layne had been on her tiptoes, and when I pulled my lips from hers, she sank back to her feet, but her hands stayed wrapped around my shoulders.

I met her blue eyes with my dark ones. They were wide, but heated. Surprised or turned on or confused, or some combination of everything.

I was feeling the same way.

I knew I liked her.

I knew I wanted her.

What I hadn't known until right now was how good it would feel to touch her, to kiss her, even just for a moment.

That was knowledge I couldn't unlearn. It was also knowledge I couldn't do anything with.

Seriously, what the hell did I do with the fact that my heart was beating out of my chest and my cock was straining?

She was someone my boss and friend trusted me to help get out of a shit situation.

Of course, what she wanted mattered more than what Jace wanted.

It was her life, after all.

But how did I find out what she actually wanted without this potentially blowing up in my face?

It was a no-win situation that could mess with my job, not to mention Layne's head since she was just getting out of a messy breakup. I cleared my throat. "I should get going." She nodded and let her arms fall. She wiped the corner of her lip with her hand, and looked anywhere but at me.

"Yeah, for sure. Thanks for the lift and everything."

I slid my feet into my boots, knowing things had shifted. "Let me know if he comes back or if you need a ride tomorrow."

She nodded. "Thanks, Elias, you're a good friend."

The word *friend* hit me like a boot to the balls.

Friends.

That's what we were.

That was how she saw me.

That was why I was doing this.

I turned and walked out the door, closing it behind me with a decisive click. The snow was still falling. It had a way of making the world silent even as my thoughts refused to shut up. I drove home on autopilot, watching for any sign of Teddy's car in case he was hanging around.

* * *

I woke up the next morning and checked my phone. There were no messages from Layne. That was a relief…sort of. I was glad I hadn't missed a message from her about Teddy, but I was hoping to hear from her anyway.

Especially after that kiss.

Friend or not, that was the hottest kiss I'd ever had. I was surprised I'd gotten to sleep with how keyed up I was from her touch. Unfortunately, rather than waking up to a beautiful woman in my bed, I had to get some work done.

It was Saturday, so technically Wild Timber Homes was closed. Realistically, we all worked whatever hours we needed to. If there was work to do, then we went in, and the Beast project was far from done. In fact, we were behind.

My phone vibrated on the nightstand, and I grabbed it fast enough that I almost dropped it on the floor.

Layne: Are you going in today?

I replied right away.

Elias: Definitely. You?

Her reply popped up quickly.

Layne: Could you give me a lift, car is snowed in.

Elias: be there in twenty

I scrubbed a hand over my face and pushed out of bed.

I really should get some distance from this woman. Then again, I couldn't just say no to someone who needed help. I set my phone aside and hit the remote start so my truck would be warm for her when I got to her place.

Yeah, I was that guy.

Whether she was in my life as a friend, a co-worker, or more, I still wanted to do things for her.

I got dressed, made a coffee, and got in the truck, pulling into her driveway a short time later. Layne was already on the porch, a pink toque pulled low over her ears. She had a to-go mug held tightly in her grip. "Nice and warm in here," she said as she slid into the passenger seat. My chest warmed that I'd taken the extra step for her.

"Any issues after I left last night?"

She shook her head, causing her blonde hair to dance around her shoulders. "I shut off my phone and went to sleep."

"Probably the smartest thing to do."

We stepped into the office to find Jace, Zane, and Wyatt already there. Wyatt looked a little green, the color of old drywall, and I stepped up next to him.

"Good morning," I said, entirely too loudly, right next to his ear.

He flinched. "Damn, man. Not so loud."

"You don't have a hangover, do you?" Layne yelled into his other ear.

Wyatt collapsed onto the couch and curled in on himself. "You're both mean."

"Just go home if you're sick," Jace said, rolling his eyes at Wyatt's theatrics.

"I never give up," he said, pushing himself off the couch.

Layne settled in behind her computer, already all business. Zane and Wyatt headed out to the yard, Wyatt shuffling like a man walking toward his own execution.

Jace pulled me aside, out of Layne's earshot. His voice dropped automatically. "Everything okay?"

"He was there when we got to her place last night," I said. "Tried to use the weather as an excuse to stay. But I got rid of him."

Jace ran a hand through his hair. "Good. Thanks." He sighed. "I don't think Layne would go back with him. I just don't want to give that little weasel a chance to try to convince her, you know?"

I nodded. "Yeah. I know."

I knew more about the whole Teddy situation than I ever wanted to.

More than was smart, maybe.

The whole thing was messing with my head.

I wanted to hold her tight. I wanted to punch him in the face. More than anything, I wanted him out of her life so she could start over, whichever way she decided to do that.

Preferably with me.

Chapter Eleven

Layne

"Jace, why is there a napkin in this pile of contracts?"

My brother gave me a sheepish look. "I was meaning to write that up. Those are my notes."

I snorted a laugh. "I'll get it written up based on your…notes, and get you to review it."

He nodded his thanks.

My brother hadn't exactly run his business in the most efficient way. He was a pen and paper kind of guy. He made deals with a handshake rather than a spreadsheet.

It was a lot of work to bring him into the current century, let alone keep up with the new work coming in.

I was happy to help him, though. I owed him that much, even if he didn't agree. Besides, the longer I was here, the more I couldn't picture going back to my job in finance.

My old job was flashier than this place. Bigger dollars, bigger risks, more pressure.

I had enjoyed the challenge. The atmosphere was corporate and clinical, even though my dad ran the business. This place was so different. It was all hands on deck, but in a neighbor helping neighbor kind of way. It was warmer, happier, less formal, and besides, Elias was here.

That shouldn't matter as much as it did.

I wasn't entirely clear if he was helping me at Jace's insistence or because he was a good guy or because he was interested in me for real. But last night had made me more sure than ever that it was the third one.

The way he had kissed me. God. There was nothing friendly about it, even if I had told him he was a good friend right after. I guess I had needed to mentally distance myself from the whole thing before I ripped off his jeans and rode his cock right there in my living room.

My life was a mess.

I had already pulled him into my chaos, but I didn't need to make it even worse. Or maybe it was too late for that.

I shook my head and refocused on my work. I didn't need to be thinking about the kiss right now. I needed to be focused on earning my keep.

But I was tired.

So much had happened in the last few months, and sometimes it hit me all at once.

"Just need to head out and check on something," Jace said, grabbing his jacket and walking out the door. I nodded. Once he was gone, I rested my head in my hands, and shut my eyes for a moment.

Having the door officially closed on Teddy and my relationship couldn't come soon enough.

The door to the office swung open a moment later, and I

jerked my head up. Elias came through the door, and the smile fell from his face. "You okay?" He asked, crossing the room to stand by my desk.

He was covered in sawdust, but I didn't call him on it.

I nodded. "Just tired, I guess."

He blew a breath out of his nose. "Come on, I'll take you home. You can take a day off once in a while."

I nodded, getting to my feet. There was no reason to fight it. I could get some work done from home later if I felt more energized.

I climbed into the passenger seat of the truck, enjoying Elias's woodsy scent. He was quiet in the driver's seat as he navigated the snowy driveway out of the lumberyard. "I wish I could do more to make this situation better for you," he admitted as he clicked on the signal light and merged into traffic.

My foolish heart gave a little squeeze. "It's not your job to fix my life, E."

He nodded. "I know. I still wish I could."

How the hell he was single, I had no idea. Although every other woman's loss could be my gain if I was brave enough to put my heart on the line when I had crashed and burned so hard with Teddy.

I zoned out for the rest of the drive until I heard Elias curse under his breath. I glanced out the windshield to see more fresh tire tracks in my driveway. "Son of a bitch. He can't possibly be here again."

We got closer to my cabin, and I saw Teddy pounding on my front door. "Your car's here. I know you are too," he yelled loud enough that I could hear him over the engine of the truck. Elias put the truck in park and got out more quickly than I did, stomping through the snow with single-minded efficiency.

I scrambled to catch up.

"What are you doing here again?" Elias demanded.

Teddy rolled his eyes dramatically. "Can I just talk to my fiancée without the guard dog?"

"I'm not your fiancée. I'm not your anything anymore, remember?"

"Whatever. Can we just talk alone, Layne? I know we can sort this out together." He flashed me what was probably supposed to be a charming smile, but it just pissed me off.

"No, we can't." If I wasn't already feeling done with this day, I sure as hell was now.

Elias wrapped an arm around my shoulders. "You heard the lady. Leave." He guided me to the front door, and we both went inside.

"I'm not leaving until you talk to me," Teddy yelled after us. I slammed the door and locked it.

Elias pulled his arm from my shoulders, and I missed his touch as soon as it was gone. "Do you want me to call the cops?" he asked.

I shook my head, feeling fully awake now. "He would charm his way out of something like that. I need a plan to get it through his head that this is over."

Chapter Twelve

Elias

Fuck, he really is persistent.

Layne had kicked off her boots and was pacing. All traces of fatigue were gone from her face, replaced by determination. "The only way to get him to really understand that we are over is for him to accept that I'm with you. We need to convince him. Really sell it."

Heat slid down my chest and lodged somewhere around my groin. The kiss we'd shared the night before had been hot. What more did she have in mind?

I glanced out the window. "He's sitting on the porch." He seems like a creature comfort kind of guy, so for him to brave the weather, he must really think he's going to win this. "You sure you don't want to get the cops involved?"

She chewed her thumbnail. Her eyes darted to the bed in the middle of the one-room cabin, then to me. A smirk sprang to her lips. "I have a better idea. Get on the bed."

My dick jumped behind my zipper.

Had I heard that right?

Layne pulled off her jacket and moved towards the bed, then turned to face me. "Come on."

I sprang into action, not sure what the hell I had just agreed to, but if it involved Layne and a bed I was, most definitely, interested.

I took off my snow boots and jacket and followed Layne, trying to keep my dick from getting hard.

"On your back," she said, gesturing to the bed.

"Can I ask what the plan is here?" I said, even as I did what she asked. My head hit her soft pillow, and the floral scent of her surrounded me. If I let my brain run with it, I could so easily picture lazy mornings in this bed with her, not to mention heated nights.

She pulled my glasses off and put them on the nightstand.

"We're going to pretend to be having sex. If seeing us kissing didn't convince him, this has to. Are you okay if I straddle you?"

I all but choked at the question. "Yes," I croaked.

Layne grabbed the throw blanket from the end of the bed. She threw her leg over my hip and settled her ass over my thighs before pulling the blanket over both of us. The blanket was huge and settled over not only our bodies but our heads too. "Why are we in a blanket fort?" I whispered.

"In case he looks in the window and sees we're dressed." The blanket rested against her head and cast an eerily pink glow in our little bubble.

I nodded. It was already getting warm under the blanket, and that was not helping me keep this in perspective. "Okay, now what?"

"Make sex noises, loud."

This was hell.

This was torture.

What did I do to deserve this?

The woman I couldn't stop thinking about was straddling me. If she moved up a little further, she'd feel me getting hard, and now she wanted me to pretend to be fucking her.

"Oh, fuck E, that's so good," she said loudly, in a breathy, strained voice.

Okay, I was wrong. *Now,* I was in hell.

How could I listen to her literally moan my name without coming in my pants like a teenager?

She poked me in the side, and I grunted. "That's better," she whispered.

"So fucking tight, baby," I yelled out, holding her gaze. She nodded, encouraging me on. "Ride me just like that."

"Yeah, that's so good," she said. She adjusted how she was sitting, moving up so her ass was nestled right over my cock. There was no way she couldn't feel how hard I was.

There was also no way I was going to get rid of this boner with her sitting in my lap.

I let out a long groan in reply, not sure what else to say.

This wasn't a porno, and having a full conversation wasn't going to sell the lie.

I pushed the top of the blanket aside enough to get my arms out and reached up to grab the slats of the headboard. The bed frame was actual wood and made by Jace, so it was solid, but we could make it move if we had to. I started pushing against the slats over and over, letting them bump the wall with a satisfying thud.

Layne's eyes lit and she leaned forward to help. She braced her hands on the slats above my head. The move put her breasts literally on my face, her stomach resting against my chest. She matched my rhythm, helping me get the bed frame to bump against the wall. The movement of her body as she pushed had her basically dry-humping me.

I let out a shaky breath as warmth licked up my spine.

The heat of her center was over my cock, and I fought the urge to capture her nipple in my mouth through the fabric of her shirt. She adjusted her position to get a better grip on the frame and gave it a proper shove. Her center dragged up the length of my dick and we both moaned in unison.

She pushed back enough for her eyes to meet mine. They were glazed with more than revenge now. There was heat there, and I was sure the same was in mine.

Again she dragged herself over me, and a drip of precum stained my boxers. I fought to keep my eyes from fluttering shut. She took her hands from the headboard entirely now, instead bracing them on my chest and rolled her hips against mine. "This okay?" she asked.

"So fucking good," I moaned, giving over to the pleasure she was giving me.

She hummed in reply, rolling her hips again. "Damn, your cock is huge."

The organ in question jumped at the praise and she kept going, moving faster, rubbing her clit over the stiff peak in the front of my jeans. We were still under our little blanket fort despite my hands being up at the headboard and sweat collected on my forehead and under my arms. Each breath felt harder to pull in than the last, but that might have been the effect of the woman currently riding me with more and more gusto.

"Hot in here," she murmured, then reached for the hem of her top, fanning it enough that I caught a glimpse of what was underneath. A lacy bra that I couldn't take my eyes off of. "Touch me, Elias," she murmured, watching me stare at her chest.

Her voice was too low to be for Teddy's benefit.

This was real.

I slid my hands under her shirt, cupping her breasts and teasing the peaks with my thumbs. "Oh, fuck, yes." Her mouth fell open, and she moved her hips faster. I was mesmerized by the sight of her over me, taking her pleasure, heat making her cheeks red, her chest flushed, her fingers curling into my pecs.

It was the hottest thing I had ever seen, and if I didn't stop this soon, I was going to make a mess.

"E, shit, I'm going to come, don't stop touching me." I did as she asked, moving my thumbs over and around her peaked nipples, drinking in the sight of her sexy body as it moved over me.

She shoved one of her hands under the tight waistband of her jeans, sliding it between her spread thighs.

Her core shook once, twice, then she let out a long, strangled moan, dropped her head between her shoulder blades and clenched her thighs around my hips. I reached between us and grabbed the base of my dick, squeezing hard before the sight of her coming sent me over the edge.

She was riding me through four layers of fabric, and still, it was almost too much to take.

Reluctantly, I let my hand fall from her chest as her body stopped shaking. Her fingers had been digging into my chest enough to leave marks through my shirt. She slid them to the side and collapsed against me. Her breast pillowed against my chest.

I threw the blanket off us, needing to cool down. If Teddy

was perving in the windows, he would see we both had pants on, but if the guy went that far then I was calling the cops, or kicking his ass myself.

I wrapped my arms around her and held her tight. I was still hard but the risk of going off like a rocket had passed. What replaced it was a bone-deep contentment that only her in my arms could bring.

I already felt protective of Layne, but as she fought to catch her breath, a surge of primal possessive need shot through my core. I wanted her to be mine.

Not pretend mine, but actually mine.

I was in too deep with her now; I knew that. I lazily ran my hand up her back, and she let out a contented sigh. I pressed my eyes shut. If she didn't want me the way I wanted her, it was going to rip me apart.

I needed to stop this now.

"Do you think he's gone?" I asked, not actually giving a shit where Teddy was.

"Who? I mean, yes. I'll check." She slid the blanket off, then climbed off my lap. I missed her weight immediately, but I needed the distance to help my dick calm down. I could feel my pre-cum sticky in my boxers as I watched her cross the room and look out the front window. She ran a hand through her hair, looking impossibly good all rumpled from what we'd just done. "His car's gone."

"Good."

Silence settled between us, but it was less awkward than I'd have thought.

I was desperate to know what had just happened between us, but with Teddy still in her life, it didn't feel like the time to ask her about starting something new.

Then again, we could have made the noises without her sitting on my lap. We could have moved the bed frame without her dry-humping me.

She could have kept her top in place and not asked me to touch her.

Did she just get carried away?

Or was she interested in me the same way I was in her?

Chapter Thirteen

Elias

Sunday morning I was restless, so after doing a load of laundry and grocery shopping, I went into work. There wasn't a ton to do until more materials arrived, but there was always something. I could do some maintenance on the chainsaws, maybe.

I pulled into the yard, not surprised to find Jace's truck already in the lot. He was one of the hardest-working people I knew, and this Beast project was taking it out of all of us. I stepped into the office to find Jace frowning down at his phone.

"What's wrong?"

He glanced up, not seeming surprised to see me. "When did you last see Layne?"

Heat crept up my cheeks. Although that was silly, there was no way he knew what Layne and I had done when I was at her house last. "Yesterday, when we were all in the office," I said. "I gave her a lift home."

Jace nodded. "She just texted to let me know that she and Teddy are meeting with the realtor tomorrow to get her name off his lease."

"That's good news, right?"

"If all goes well, it is. She mentioned that he showed up at her place after the barbecue on Friday and again yesterday. Do you think you could..."

"What?"

"I know you guys are pretending to be dating. Any chance you could go over there tonight, stay there with her, to make sure Teddy doesn't try to do something stupid?"

I hesitated.

He went on. "She'd never accept me hanging around, but she trusts you."

I ran my hand over the back of my neck. I was in too deep. I had to tell him. "I've got to talk to you about that, actually."

Jace's brow dropped. "What's wrong?"

"Look, she's your sister, and you're my boss and my friend. I think of her as my friend too, but...I'm starting to see her as more." Jace continued to stare, so I clarified. "I think I have feelings for her."

"And how does she feel about you?" he asked, gently.

After my concerns of him being pissed off, this was a good start.

I shrugged. "I don't know, honestly. This whole fake-dating thing has made the water kind of muddy. Besides, she's not completely done with her ex yet, so now would be a really bad time to start asking her hard questions."

He nodded. "First of all, she is one hundred percent done with her ex. The fact that they still have their names on a lease doesn't mean she feels a damn thing for that guy."

"I know that," I said. "I just mean she's got enough drama coming from one guy. She doesn't need anything from me besides support."

He nodded. "You know I'm protective of my sister, but you also know I pretended not to have feelings for Sloane from the time we were teenagers until just a few months ago."

I hadn't really thought about the similarities between Jace's experience with love and what was going on in my head about Layne.

"I wasted a lot of time because I made assumptions. I thought Layne wouldn't approve of me dating her friend. I thought Sloane wouldn't be interested in a guy like me. Turns out I was wrong on both fronts, and I'm happy to have been wrong." He leaned back in his seat, staring off. "Sloane makes me happy in a way I never thought I could be, in a way I never thought I wanted. I wouldn't say this to just anyone, but I know you, and I trust you. If you think there can be something between the two of you, you need to let her know. Layne's a big girl. If she's not interested, she'll say so, and you guys will move on. But if she is, you might just find more than you think you deserve, or more than you thought you were looking for too."

I left the office with a new sense of determination in my chest. I pulled out my phone and texted Layne.

Elias: I heard you have a meeting with Teddy tomorrow.

She messaged me back right away.

Layne: Assuming he shows, I do.

I took a deep breath, not knowing exactly what to say. Shit, maybe I should have just called her.

Elias: Can I come over tonight? Just in case he shows up again.

Three dots appeared on the screen, and I held my breath until the message appeared. It was one word.

Layne: Sure.

I wasn't one for grand gestures, for expensive gifts and roses and chocolates, but I was sure Layne knew that about me. All I could do was be me and see if that was enough. I'd go there tonight to make sure Teddy didn't show up, but I wouldn't show up just to be there. I'd show her how I felt, how things could be between us if she wanted to take the risk with me.

I went home and showered, roughly forming a plan in my head as I cleaned my skin. I hadn't even done any work when I'd gone to the office, but even just wearing my work jacket meant I probably smelled a little like gas or oil.

Dressing in what I would consider my nicer clothes: jeans without rips or stains and a shirt that actually had buttons. I touched up my closely buzzed hair and beard. Once I was ready, I stepped out into the cold and drove to the supermarket to grab a few things.

Once I had everything I needed, I drove the now familiar route to Layne's cabin.

I could make her dinner, and then we could talk.

By the end of the night, one way or another, I would know where we stood.

Chapter Fourteen

Layne

"I'm freaking out," I yelled into the phone as soon as Sloane answered.

"Uh, okay, context please."

"It's Elias," I ran a hand through my hair and sank down onto my bed.

"What did that fucker—"

"No, no, not like that. It's good. At least, I think it's good." I explained what had happened since I'd seen her on Friday night, well, a PG version of it, anyway.

I'd wanted to ask him to stay that night, but I'd been a little overwhelmed to feel so much for him so soon after things ended with Teddy. Elias was just so easy to be around. So easy to trust. The antithesis of all the things that had driven me to cancel my wedding.

And maybe I'd been embarrassed too. I'd begged my co-worker to let me ride him, to tease my nipples, and then I came while writhing on his cock.

I refocused on my conversation with Sloane.

"Now, a day later, he asked to come over, and I said yes, but all my feelings are bubbling to the surface. He will probably spend the night, and I only have one bed, and I don't know what to do..."

"Yes, you do." Her voice was slow and patient.

"What? No. Sloane, I'm calling for advice because I don't know what to do."

"You don't want advice, you want permission. Teddy was an ass; he made your brother miserable. The wedding cost a fortune, and a lot of people put work into it, then it didn't happen. You want to move on from him and what happened, but you feel bad."

"That's not it," I said quickly, too quickly maybe. I started to pace, something I did a lot lately.

"Really, then why are you working so many hours for Jace's company when you don't have to?" I winced as her words hit home. "More importantly, why are you keeping Elias at arm's length even though you are both adults who clearly like each other?"

"He's Jace's employee and his friend..." I whined.

"And I am your friend, and now dating your brother. And what was your reaction when I told you that?"

"I mean, I was happy for you guys, of course."

"If you care about people, you want them to be happy," she cut in. "Jace cares about you."

"I know," I said quietly, sitting on the side of the bed and picking at the edge of my blanket. The same blanket I'd thrown over Elias and I the day before. I brought it to my nose, still smelling a hint of fresh-cut pine on the fabric.

"You have to decide what you want. Not what you think other people want for you. Not what you think you deserve after your last relationship went belly up. I'm not going to tell you what to do, but I think you know what's right."

After we hung up, I sat with her words. She was my friend; she wouldn't have said the things she did if she didn't think they were true. I did feel guilty about how Teddy treated Jace. I did feel bad that so many people had provided money and help towards my wedding, and then I'd called it off.

Was that part of why I was keeping things with Elias from being more?

Why I hadn't asked him if he wanted to go from pretend to real even after what happened last night? I knew my brother forgave me; my family understood. Sloane was still here with me even after the things that had happened. Maybe tonight I could put my past aside and enjoy Elias's company. See things for what they were without the weight of a past relationship shaping my feelings.

There was a knock at the door, and my time was up to figure out what to do.

I opened the door, and a gust of cold wind swept into the room, making my skin prickle. Elias stood there looking unfairly good in a simple pair of jeans and a jacket, holding a grocery bag in each hand. "What's all this?"

He shrugged. "Figure maybe I can scare Teddy off with my terrible cooking skills." He moved into my cabin, his pine smell coming with him, and kicked off his boots.

I laughed and took the bags to the kitchen. He came to stand beside me, unloading groceries onto the counter and washing his hands. "What are you going to make?" I tried to remember if Teddy ever cooked for me, then shoved that thought aside;

this wasn't about him.

"Pasta with shrimp in a creamy pesto sauce, the only dish with more than three ingredients I can make. How's that sound?"

"Amazing," I said honestly, my shoulder bumping his as I started peeling garlic.

"It will be if I can pull it off. Otherwise, we'll fill up on garlic bread and wine."

"That should be plan A." I grabbed the bottle of wine from the counter and poured us each a glass.

We joked as we worked side by side, our arms brushing just often enough to have my skin tingling with awareness. It was dark outside the window, cold with a bit of snow falling, but inside the cabin it was warm and bright, smelling of pine and garlic.

Despite his saying he couldn't cook, it smelled amazing and within a short time we had dinner ready to eat.

We settled in at the table, wine glasses refilled and a pot of pasta between us big enough to feed twice as many people. He had his sleeves rolled up to his elbows and his forearm flexed as he stirred the pot. He dished some onto my plate, making sure I got lots of shrimp, then filled his own. "Should we toast to something?" I asked.

"Sure, how about a toast to carbs?" He took an exaggerated bite of garlic bread.

I laughed. I had been thinking a toast to fresh starts. To friends becoming more. To realizing what really mattered. But I like his toast better. It was simple and honest. I picked up my glass. "To carbs," I clinked my glass against his and started twirling pasta around my fork. I could feel him watching me, so I took a huge bite. The taste hit my tongue, and I moaned. "Oh my god, this is amazing." I turned to look at him; his mouth was hanging open with his fork halfway to his mouth.

"That was…quite the reaction."

I blushed and laughed as I chewed. "Just showing my appreciation to the chef." In my old life, the years I was with Teddy, we kept things pretty formal. No coffee in our pajamas or pizza nights in front of the TV. I enjoyed it at the time. I thought it was what grown-ups did. But this, joking about carbs and letting my appreciation for the taste really show, this was better.

"I wasn't sure if I should have made a garlic dish," he said, wiping a spot of sauce off his chin.

"Garlic is always the answer for future reference." It really was delicious.

He shrugged, staring determinedly at his plate. "I was just hoping I'd need fresh breath for something after dinner was over." He glanced up at me, pink tinging his cheeks.

I paused, a half-eaten piece of garlic bread in my fingers. I thought back to the things Sloane had said earlier about me holding on to guilt. About how I had to give myself permission to let this man in. "You definitely will. But I have lots of toothpaste."

Chapter Fifteen

Elias

Nerves jangled in my stomach as we finished our meal.

I had been unsure how she actually saw me.

I had worried about Jace's opinion and about her still disentangling her life from Teddy's.

But Jace wasn't going to castrate me for touching his sister, Teddy was too annoying to worm his way back into her life, and Layne had been looking at me over her dinner like she'd rather eat me than the garlic bread.

This was actually happening, and I was equally excited and nervous. It felt different from other dates. Bigger or more important somehow. Like she might be the last woman I ever kissed.

The last one I ever wanted to.

We finished eating and stood at the counter, again side by side, washing dishes and putting them away. It felt different now than it had when we were cooking. Then I had been anticipating dinner; now, I was anticipating her.

"So, I'm going to go brush my teeth," she said, giving me a significant look before heading to the bathroom.

Garlic breath was a weird thing to flirt about, but I wasn't exactly a romance expert.

Cooking dinner was about as complicated as I knew how to get. But I wasn't trying to impress the old Layne, and this new one didn't seem to want complicated.

Once she was done, I slipped into the bathroom myself and did some quick pre-sex prep.

When I came out, she was sitting on the edge of the bed. I took a deep breath, taking her in. Her blonde hair was pulled back into a loose ponytail. She was wearing jeans and a T-shirt, nothing fancy, just her.

Or the version of her that lived in a cabin in the woods. I didn't know the finance executive version of her that almost married Teddy. I suspected that person was gone, anyway. I needed to focus on the person right in front of me.

She patted the bed next to her, and I moved across the room.

"No one here to pretend for," I said, sitting beside her close enough that our thighs touched.

She nodded. "I don't want to fake anything with you. Not anymore. Not after you fed me pasta."

I smirked. "If I had known all it took was carbs, I would have brought you a loaf of bread the first time we met."

She sucked in a breath. "Did you want me back then?" She shuffled closer.

I nodded. "But not as much as now. Now that we've spent some time together, including with you writhing on top of me, you're all I can think about."

She reached her hand out to cup my jaw. "Me too."

She leaned in, closing the last of the distance between us, and her mouth was on mine. She tasted like toothpaste, smelled like heaven, and I eased her onto her back before climbing onto the bed over her.

I propped myself up on my elbows so I didn't squish her as I explored her mouth with mine.

There was nothing frantic in the way we moved. It was just us. It felt like a long time coming, but also like we had all the time in the world. I didn't want to rush something I knew I would remember forever.

Layne didn't seem to be feeling as sentimental as I was.

As soon as I lay over her, she slid her hand between us and palmed my length through my jeans. I let out a grunt, as if I'd been punched; her touch was better than anything I'd ever felt. Her lips stilled under mine as she concentrated on getting my button open and lowering my zipper.

Once she had them down, she brought her legs up and hooked her toes into the waistband of my jeans and shoved them down my legs. I laughed against her lips.

"Do you want me to just save you some trouble and strip?"

"That would be great, actually," she said, leaning back on her elbows and watching me as I pushed myself from the bed and kicked my jeans off my feet. I set my glasses on the nightstand, then slid my flannel off my shoulders and pulled my shirt over my head. I couldn't see her as well now, but I knew her eyes were on me as I took off my boxers and stood naked before her.

"Get back here," she said, her voice having taken on a gravelly quality I hadn't heard before.

I settled between her thighs and ran my hands reverently down her arms.

"You know how badly I wanted to ride you when you were

here the other day? Making the noises and the motions when I wanted to strip us both down and go at it for real?"

I groaned at her words and thrust against her core, cursing the fact that she was still wearing clothes. "God, I wanted that too. Take these off."

She grunted and swore as she shimmied her jeans down her hips and off her feet. Her shirt went next. I made things harder when I leaned down and sucked her nipple into my mouth through the lace of her bra. She arched up into my touch while still trying to work her panties down her legs.

"Next time we strip first," she said, panting.

"So there will be a next time?" I asked, resting my chin on her ribs and looking up into her face.

"There will definitely be a next time. Now help me get this thing off."

Chapter Sixteen

Elias

Between the two of us, we managed to get her naked, and then all bets were off. I gripped her smooth thighs in my hands, kissing her hard. Then I shoved her knees up toward her shoulders and dove headfirst between her thighs. The sun had set while we were cleaning up, and the only light was coming from the kitchen. She was partly in shadow, but without my glasses my vision was blurry anyway.

"Going to make you come so hard," I murmured before running my tongue over her center.

Her breath caught, and I did it again, teasing between her folds, then circling that little bundle of nerves. I worked her clit for a minute, loving the little noises she made, then sank lower, spearing my tongue inside her, thrusting in and out.

Her hands came to rest on the buzzed hair on the top of my head, and she slid her fingers over the short strands. I rested my hands on the insides of her knees, holding her wide open for me to feast on.

I wanted to leave her breathless, to make her come hard and fast, to have her clamp her thighs around my ears as I gave her a finish like she'd never had.

With that in mind, I sucked her clit hard. The way she cried out was music to my ears, so I kept at it, sucking hard then sliding into her with my tongue. I shoved the messy blankets out of the way, then moved one hand up to tease her bare breasts. She thrust her hips up to meet my face before every muscle in her body tightened, and she was coming.

"Holy shit, Elias," she murmured as she rode my face, drawing out every drop of pleasure I could give her. When she sank back to the mattress, I pulled back, wiping my mouth with my hand and bringing my chest down to rest against hers. I kissed her, softer this time, slower, even as my throbbing cock twitched against her stomach.

"How do you want it?" I asked.

"However. I just want you."

"Protection?"

She shook her head. "I have condoms, but I'm clean and on the pill."

"I'm clean too."

She smirked. "Then let's do this without."

I grabbed her thigh and yanked it over, flipping her onto her stomach. Her ass was a perfect curve that I ran my hand over before pulling her hips back and lining my cock up with her entrance. I was dripping precum, desperate to feel her and in shock that this was happening at all. I channeled all of that feeling into pressing myself against her entrance and slowly sliding inside.

She let out a groan, or maybe it was me. Her heat hugging me was perfect. My hips resting against the curve of her ass was like nothing I had felt before.

Then I started to move. Shallow at first, slowly. Her skin against mine was warm and soft. The smell of her was all around me. The cabin could be in the middle of a city, in the middle of the forest, or on the moon. It didn't matter because it was just the two of us. And this time it wasn't a performance. We weren't doing it to scare away Teddy. We were doing it because we wanted to. To mark the start of something new.

Layne thrust her hips back, clearly impatient with the pace I'd set. I gripped her hips harder, my thumbs digging into the muscle at the top of her ass cheeks, and I picked up the pace. Rather than leisurely thrusting in and out, I snapped my hips hard, hitting her as deep as I could go. The moan she made let me know this was exactly what she wanted. Over and over, I snapped my hips, holding her tight, not wanting to let her go. She took everything I threw at her and groaned for more.

She was perfect.

Heat built at the base of my spine, fire licking up the backs of my thighs, and I knew this wasn't going to last. With her on her stomach, I wasn't sure if I could work her clit, but I tried anyway. I wedged one hand under her body and found that spot. I circled it repeatedly as I thrust. My technique was sloppy, but based on the sound she was making, I didn't think it mattered.

"Elias, I'm close," she said, her voice sounding strained as she buried her face into the pillow.

"Me too, honey, me too."

I concentrated on the simple motion of it. My finger going in a circle, my hips pulling back and forth. My lower back felt the strain, my thighs quaked, and the one arm that was holding up my weight trembled. It was all the perfect distraction so I could get her off before I fell over the edge myself. She ground her hips down against my hand a few times, and her inner muscles clenched around me as she came again.

"Oh, shit."

The movement of my hips went off rhythm. It was too much. The hug of her inner muscles around my cock as she came was the last straw before I tumbled over the edge myself. My cock throbbed and pulsed inside her, filling her, claiming her.

Being with her was different than being with anyone else. We knew each other as friends before we knew each other as anything else. In some ways, we even practiced the physical before we got to do it for real. Because of that, our first time together was more. There was no awkward fumbling, no barrier between us. I marked her, gripping her hips, and filling her.

I could feel her chest rising and falling rapidly under me and I pulled carefully out before letting my arm collapse and falling on my side next to her on the mattress. I was worn out. I felt like I'd run a marathon, but in the best possible way. I reached my hand over and ran it reverently over her bare skin, down the curve of her spine and over the globes of her ass. She was perfect. Beautiful and strong, and if I was reading the situation right, she was also mine.

Chapter Seventeen

Layne

We fell asleep like that. Just the two of us, naked in the bed together.

I was satisfied in a way I couldn't begin to describe. I'd never compare one lover to another, not out loud anyway. But much like everything else with Elias, it was perfect because it was simple and real. No lit candles or fancy lingerie. No performative dirty talk or pricey wine. The only set-up required was a toothbrush and the shedding of clothes. The only thing we needed was us and our bare skin.

I had come to live in this cabin to lick my wounds, to distance myself from Teddy, and to figure out what I wanted to do with my life. But now that I was here, I couldn't picture myself leaving. I didn't want to go back to wearing heels and a suit every day. I didn't want to work with high-power clients. I liked the day-to-day of helping Jace run his small business. I liked the intimacy of a small town, the way people saw *me* instead of my résumé. And most importantly, I liked falling asleep with Elias's strong arms around me.

That realization settled deep in my chest, equal parts comfort and fear. There was an importance to what I felt for Elias that was bigger than anything that came before it. But I knew it was worth the risk.

I woke up the next morning already running late. I hadn't thought to set an alarm, but I wanted to meet the realtor in hopes that Teddy would show up.

This had to be the end of it. I wanted Elias to know how I felt about him. I didn't want him to worry for one moment that Teddy was the reason I wanted to be with him.

Elias was still asleep next to me, and I lingered for a moment even though I needed to get moving. He looked peaceful in sleep, and unfairly sexy in my bed. He was on his side with one well-muscled arm around my waist, his chest bare. I now knew exactly what it felt like to run my fingers through the dark hair that grew there.

My future with him was starting now, but I still wanted all of Teddy in the past.

Reluctantly, I slid out of bed and took a quick shower before getting dressed.

When I came back out to the kitchen, Elias was standing in front of the coffee maker wearing just a pair of jeans.

"Morning."

I crossed the room and wrapped by arms around him from behind, pressing my cheek to the warm skin between his shoulders. "Morning, you made coffee."

He shrugged, holding my arm around him. "Can't start a day without it. Are you going to meet Teddy this morning?"

I pulled away so I wouldn't get lost in him again. "I hope so.

He's supposed to show up. If this goes well, this is the last time I have to see him."

The weight in my chest eased at the thought, only to tighten again when there was a knock on my front door. Elias and I made eye contact before I crossed the room to answer it.

Elias leaned against the countertop and watched, not stepping in. That trust—that quiet confidence that I could handle this—steadied me more than anything he could've said.

"Morning, Teddy. I thought we were meeting at the real estate office." I looked him over. "What are you wearing?"

He stood there in a tuxedo and dress shoes, wildly inappropriate for the snow, holding a bouquet of roses like a prop.

"Layne, I tried to get you alone and you refused every time. So I'm saying what I need to say now." He took a measured breath, the same one he used before presentations at work. "You and I met working for your dad's company. High dollars. High power. This place isn't you. Our condo is. Granite. Leather. City views. You need to come home."

I didn't interrupt him. I just watched.

It struck me how little he'd changed. Same cadence. Same certainty. Same belief that reality would fall in line with whatever he wanted.

"I get that you like this rustic thing," he continued, gesturing dismissively to my cozy cabin. "You can visit Jace whenever you want. Fill our place with handmade furniture. I'll adjust."

I took a breath. "The life I'm building here isn't a phase or a tantrum or an aesthetic. It's not a way to get your attention. It's a correction. It's a return to the things that used to make me happy before I got carried away with all the things money could buy."

I glanced back at Elias, who was watching the interaction

intently.

"Layne, your career—"

"I know you think being with me will put you in line to take over my dad's company." My voice stayed calm. "You still have that chance. My dad is a fair man, and there is one less person vying for the top position because I'm not going back."

His jaw tightened. "I don't know who you are in this place. This isn't you."

I shook my head. "You're right, you don't know me in this place. I've changed and you haven't. That's why we will never be together again."

His nostrils flared and I could see the wheels turning, thinking of something to change my mind.

I continued, not wanting to give him the change. "I love my job here. I have my brother. My friends." I met Elias's eyes. "And I have a boyfriend who sees me for who I am. Can you just be happy for me, and let me move on?"

He looked around the cabin, clearly seeing boring where I saw belonging.

"Go put on a jacket," I said. "Put on boots. Meet me at the real estate office in a half hour. We'll sign the papers and be done."

I closed the door before he could respond.

I turned to Elias. He crossed the room but stopped short, hands in his pockets.

"I'm going to sign the last paper I need to officially have Teddy out of my life," I said.

"Okay."

"Since I'm monologuing this morning, I'll make one more. I don't know when this stopped being pretend, just that it isn't anymore. The things I've said and done with you, whether in front of Teddy or when we're alone, I meant them. All of them."

His face softened. "It never felt like an act to me." He pulled me closer. "You used the word *boyfriend*," he added carefully. "Did you mean it?"

I nodded. "Assuming you'll have me?"

His grin was slow and real. "Of course I will."

"Good. I've had enough of performative relationships to last a lifetime. I just want something honest and real."

He brushed his thumb along my jaw. "Then stay honest and stay here with me."

I wrapped my arms around him, resting my forehead against his chest.

"This is a big change for you. Any regrets?" he asked.

"Not a single one."

Outside, the snow kept falling. A steady backdrop to the start of something new.

I had come here to heal. I hadn't expected to stay. I hadn't expected to fall for someone again. But sometimes endings aren't endings at all. Some are beginnings if you're brave enough to choose them.

Epilogue - Four Months Later

Layne

The Beast project was still moving along, with more bumps and interruptions than any project I had ever seen. Because of that, I had been frowning at our work schedule, trying to move things around so the delays weren't felt on the client end. I didn't mind. I never had. I was with my brother and my friends here. More importantly, I was with Elias.

I had gone to the real estate office that day after Elias and I had confessed our feelings for each other in my kitchen. Teddy had put on boots and a jacket, as I'd suggested. His face had been blank, and he hadn't said a word to me as he signed on the dotted line to cancel our lease before he walked out the door, and didn't look back.

I hadn't asked about him when I saw my parents, and they hadn't talked about him. He was in the past, and my future was here. No more heels and luxury cars. Now it was all about sawdust and true love.

Normally there would have been chainsaws running in the yard, but there had been a materials delay on the Beast project, so we were all waiting patiently for what we needed to do more of the finishing work.

That kept me busy with planning and Jace busy with worrying.

The door opened and a woman came bustling through. She looked harried and was juggling a file of papers in her hand. Her hair was falling out of a ponytail and her purse slid off her shoulder as she came in.

"Can I help you?"

It was odd for a customer to come into the office without calling or emailing, but not unheard of. She dropped everything she was holding onto my desk and sank into the chair. She pushed a stray strand of hair from her mouth.

"Please tell me you have a carpenter who can help me design a nightstand."

I blinked at her. "Well, we build log homes, but we do some side work here and there. What did you have in mind?"

She set her purse aside. "Picture this," she raised her hands as if she were actually drawing it. "You have family over for dinner and your toddler wanders off, then suddenly they return to the kitchen with your vibrator in their hands. How embarrassing."

I cocked an eyebrow at her. "I'm not sure how a home-building company can help with that."

She deflated. "I want to design a nightstand with a hidden compartment for sex toys. A way to keep your fun stuff handy, but not so handy that your kids can get their hands on them. See what I mean?"

I nodded, still confused. "But?"

"But I need to see it, you know. I haven't figured out how to have the hidden compartment work. I need a carpenter who is used to thinking outside the box. Do you have someone who can help?"

I bit my lip to keep from smiling. My mind flicked to Wyatt who loved to stir up trouble and had been teasing Elias and I non stop since we got together.

"I have just the guy for the job."

I grabbed a piece of paper and a pen and handed it to her. "Give me your name and contact info and I'll get him to call you."

"You're a life saver," she said, beaming.

She handed me the paper and bustled back out of the office.

A while later Elias and Wyatt came through. I flashed them both a grin. "What's that look for?" Wyatt asked, "not more changes?"

I shook my head. "Nope, a side project for you. Customer wanting to build a custom nightstand. Should be easy. Keep you out of trouble until more materials arrive." He took the paper from my hands and shrugged. "Cool, thanks, can always use the extra cash."

Elias came around the desk and leaned down to kiss me, sawdust stuck in the stubble on his chin and I wiped it away. "Ready to go home?"

I nodded and grabbed my things.

We walked out the door with his arm around my shoulders.

It was spring now. The ground was thawing, and mud squished under my boots as we walked away from the office.

"Do I want to know what that was about?"

I laughed. "Just a little payback." I explained the situation, and Elias laughed and pulled me closer to his side.

The cabin I had moved into after I'd called off my wedding was one that Jace had built with the intention of selling. He'd insisted I move into it while I sorted out my life, but once Elias and I were together, I moved in with him. It freed up Jace's cabin so he could sell it, and it meant I could wake up to the man I loved every day.

He started up the truck, and we drove out of the yard in the direction of home. He rested his hand on my knee, as he always did when he was driving, and I let the warmth sink into my skin.

"So you've lived it, an entire season in Wildrose Bend?" he said, glancing at me from the corner of his eye.

I nodded.

"Any regrets?"

I laughed. "You asked me that the last day that I had to see Teddy, and I'll tell you the same thing I told you then. I don't have a single regret about any of this. Not even about Teddy. If I hadn't met him, if I hadn't seen a person who embodied just how soulless and surface-level the life I was living had been, I wouldn't have fully appreciated the life I built here. The one I've built with you."

He looked at me and smiled like he always did. Like he still couldn't quite believe I was here.

I smiled back, because neither could I.

He squeezed my knee, and I turned to look out the window, watching the trees go by. I knew that once we got home, we would make dinner together. Something simple. Maybe we'd watch some TV or read a book, and then fall into bed together. He'd curl his chest against my back and wrap his arm around my waist, holding me like I was the only thing in the world that mattered. We'd sleep until our alarm went off and then get up and go to work together, and do it all again the next day.

It was simple and routine, and the most beautiful life I could have imagined. Maybe every minute of it didn't sparkle like gold, but to me it was even more precious.

I had come to Wildrose Bend for a break. Instead, I'd started something brand new.

I had come here to recover from a broken engagement. Instead, I found the kind of love that didn't need to be staged or polished to be real.

Enjoying your stay in Wildrose Bend? Find out if Wyatt finds love in Rough Cut Romance, available on Amazon now!

Check out my full catalog!

Highway of Love Series

Tow the Line
A Wrench in the Plan
For the Long Haul
Go the Extra Mile
Going the Distance
The Wheels Fall Off

Strawberry Hill Search and Rescue Series

A Rescue for the Mountain Man
A Detour for the Mountain Man
A New Start for the Mountain Man

Vegas Vows

Beauty and the Builder
Grease and Glamour
Pretty in Paint

Check out my full catalog!

Wild Timber Homes

Lumber and Lace
Rough Cut Romance
Wood you be Mine

Sage Valley Standalones

Mr. Write
Just Screwing Around
Making a Mountain Man

Christmas

Snowed in with the Blue-Collar Billionaire
Teaching Christmas to the Mountain Man

Multi-Author Series

Her Protective Biker
Unplanned Mountain Man
Butting Heads with the Bodyguard
Felled by the Lumberjack

Alana Gray

Writer of Rugged Romance

About the Author

Alana Gray is a Canadian writer hoping to prove that romance doesn't end when you turn thirty.

She lives in the interior of British Columbia with her husband, daughter, and one sassy cat. These beautiful surroundings inspire blue-collar characters, unpredictable weather, and forced proximity sparks to fly.

Visit www.AuthorAlanaGray.com to see my full list of books!

www.ingramcontent.com/pod-product-compliance
Lightning Source LLC
LaVergne TN
LVHW051015080826
845145LV00009B/2629

* 9 7 8 1 0 6 9 8 1 2 0 8 7 *